THE USBORNE BOOK OF
CASTLE TALES

Heather Amery
Illustrated by Stephen Cartwright

Language consultant: Betty Root
Series editor: Jenny Tyler

There is a little yellow duck to find

D1165253

Notes for parents

The stories in this delightful picture book are ones which your child will want to share with you many times.

All the stories in *Castle Tales* have been written in a special way to ensure that young children succeed in their first efforts to read.

To help with that success, first read the whole of one story aloud and talk about the pictures. Then encourage your child to read the short, simpler text at the top of each page and read the longer text at the bottom of the page yourself. This turn about reading builds up confidence and children do love joining in. It is a great day when they discover that they can read a whole story for themselves.

Castle Tales provides an enjoyable opportunity for parents and children to share the excitement of learning to read.

Betty Root

THE PRINCESS
AND THE PIG

This is Grey Stone Castle.

This is King Leo and Queen Rose. They have two children called Prince Max and Princess Alice.

Max and Alice are playing outside.

They have lots of old clothes for dressing up.
They are playing at being kings and queens.

"What's that?" asks Alice.

"There's something in that big puddle."
"It's a small pig,"says Max. "It can't get out."

Alice picks up the pig.

"Poor little pig," she says. "He must have escaped from the sty. And now he's all muddy and wet."

"Now you are all muddy too," says Max.

"Don't let Queen Mama see you. She told you this morning not to get your dress dirty."

"I'll go indoors," says Alice.

She carries the little pig into the castle.
Alice finds a bath and puts the pig in it.

Alice fetches some water.

She goes to the well and fills two buckets with
water. Then she carries them back to the castle.

Alice puts the water in the bath.

She finds some soap and a brush. She washes
the pig all over. The bubbles make him sneeze.

The pig is very clean now.

Alice lifts him out of the bath. She dries him with a towel. The pig tries to run away.

The Queen comes in.

"Where did you get that pig? And why are you dirty?" she says. "Just look at your dress."

Alice holds up the pig.

"I found him in a puddle," she says. "He's such a pretty pig." She kisses him on his snout.

There is a big flash of light.

"What was that?" asks Alice. She looks at the pig.
He isn't a pig now. He has turned into a prince.

"Can't he stay with us?" says Max.

"No," says the Queen. "We can't have a strange prince in the castle. Change him back at once."

Alice kisses the prince.

There is a flash of light. The prince has turned
into a pig again. "That's better," says the Queen.

"Take him back to the sty."

"And don't kiss him again," says the Queen.
"No," says Alice. "I like pigs better than princes."

THE LITTLE
DRAGON

This is Grey Stone Castle.

This is King Leo and Queen Rose. They have two children called Prince Max and Princess Alice.

Max and Alice are playing outside.

Max is a knight and Alice is a dragon. "Let's go
and find a real dragon," says Max.

They go out of the castle gate.

"We're going to find a dragon," says Alice.
"There aren't any dragons," says the guard.

They walk across the bridge.

Then Max and Alice walk along the road up a hill.
"Will we find a real dragon?" says Alice.

"There's a cave," says Max.

"Dragons live in caves. I hope we find a dragon in it." "I wish King Dad was here," says Alice.

They look into the cave.

"Come out, dragon," shouts Max. He waves his sword. "There's nothing there," says Alice.

"Look at that," says Max.

A puff of smoke and flames come out of the cave.
"Let's go home now," says Alice.

"What do you want?"

A dragon walks out. "I was asleep. You woke me up," he says. He yawns and shows his teeth.

"You don't scare me."

"I am a princess," says Alice."You are only a small dragon. So don't be so cross and grumpy."

"Sorry," says the dragon.

He bows his head. "I'm so hungry. Every time I ask anyone for food, they run away," he says.

"Come with us," says Max.

They walk down the hill. The dragon runs after them. "Wait for me," he says.

Max and Alice go back to the castle.

The King comes out. "What's that?" he says.
Old Gus, a servant, hides behind the door.

"It's a very hungry dragon."

"Bring a very large dragon breakfast, please,"
says the King to Old Gus.

"Here comes your food," says Max.

Old Gus brings a huge plate of food. He puts it on the ground. "Thank you," says the dragon.

"May we keep him, please?" says Alice.

"Yes," says the King. "He can have three meals a day and light the castle fires for us."

THE ROYAL BROOMSTICK

This is Grey Stone Castle.

This is King Leo and Queen Rose. They have two children called Prince Max and Princess Alice.

Today it is raining.

"What shall we do?" says Max. "Let's go up to see Queen Gran in her tower," says Alice.

Max and Alice climb the stairs to the tower.

The room is empty. "Where's Queen Gran?"
asks Alice. "She must have gone out," says Max.

"There's a broomstick."

"Let's pretend it's a horse," says Alice. "Queen Gran says we musn't touch anything," says Max.

Alice gets on the broomstick.

"Look, Max, it's moving. Quick, get on," says Alice. The broomstick flies around the room.

"What shall we do?"

"Hold on tight," says Max. They fly out of the
window and around the top of the tower.

"Where are we going?"

"How do you steer a broomstick?" asks Max.
"I don't know but I'm not scared," says Alice.

The broomstick flies on.

It flies near a very tall tree. "Look!" says Max.
"I can see something moving in the tree."

"It's Lucky, Queen Gran's cat."

"Poor Lucky is stuck and she can't get down," says Alice. The broomstick stops near the cat.

The cat jumps on.

"Hold on, Lucky," says Alice. "You're safe now."
"Take us home please, broomstick," says Max.

They all fly back to the castle.

The broomstick whizzes through the window and stops. Max, Alice and Lucky jump off.

"That was fun," says Max.

"Quick, put the broomstick back in the corner,"
says Alice. "I can hear someone coming."

Queen Gran comes in.

"There you are, my dears," she says. "I hope you have been good and not touched anything."

"Oh! There's Lucky."

"I have been looking for her everywhere,"
says Queen Gran. "I thought she was lost."

"We've been a little naughty."

"But we did find Lucky," says Max. "It was
the broomstick which found her," says Alice.

THE
TOURNAMENT

This is Grey Stone Castle.

This is King Leo and Queen Rose. They have two children called Prince Max and Princess Alice.

Today everyone is busy.

"What's happening?" says Max. "I'm having a grand tournament tomorrow," says the King.

"What's a tournament?" asks Alice.

"Knights on horses fight each other," says the King. "It will happen down there on the field."

"I'm going on my pony."

"I'm going to play at being a knight," says
Max. He runs to the stables. Alice follows him.

"Can I come?" asks Alice.

"No," says Max. "Only boys can be knights."
He gets on his pony and rides away.

Alice runs to Max's bedroom.

She puts on Max's old clothes and a cap over her hair. "Now I look like a boy," she says.

Alice goes to the stables.

She gets on a pony and rides down to the field. Max is pretending to be a knight.

"Come and play," says a boy.

"You can play at being a knight. You must have a helmet, a shield and a wooden lance."

"What's your name?"

"Um, it's Alex," Alice tells the boy. She puts on the helmet. "Here's your shield," says the boy.

"Come on, come and fight."

A big boy shouts at Alice. Alice rides up to
the rails and holds up her lance and shield.

"I'll knock you off."

The big boy shouts. He rides at Alice. He tries to hit her with his lance. But he misses her.

Alice swings her lance.

She hits the big boy when he rides past.
He falls off his pony. "I've won!" shouts Alice.

"It's my turn."

"Come and fight me," shouts Max. But Alice's pony stumbles and Alice falls off.

The King and Queen come and look.

"Is that boy hurt?" asks the Queen. She takes off Alice's helmet. "Oh, it's Alice!" she says.

The King picks up Alice.

"You're a very naughty girl," says the Queen.
"You're a brave little knight," says the King.

First published in 1996 by Usborne Publishing Ltd, 83-85 Saffron Hill, London EC1N 8RT, England. Copyright © 1996 Usborne Publishing Ltd. The name Usborne and the device 🐝 are Trade Marks of Usborne Publishing Ltd. All rights reserved. No part of this publication may be reproduced, stored in a retrieval system, or transmitted in any form or by any means, electronic, mechanical, photocopy, recording or otherwise, without prior permission of the publisher. UE First published in America in August 1996. Printed in Italy.